I PICKED A FLOWER

WRITTEN AND ILLUSTRATED BY SHARON LERNER

LERNER PUBLICATIONS COMPANY
MINNEAPOLIS, MINNESOTA

Copyright © 1967 by Lerner Publications Company.

All rights reserved. International copyright secured. Manufactured in the United States of America. Published simultaneously in Canada by J. M. Dent & Sons Ltd., Don Mills, Ontario.

International Standard Book Number: 0-8225-0261-5
Library of Congress Catalog Card Number: 67-15699

Third Printing 1973

CONTENTS

Introduction 5
Daffodil 8
Rose 10
Daisy 12
Tulip 14
Geranium 16
Snapdragon 18
Pansy 20
Poppy 22
Lily of the Valley 24
Sunflower 26
Zinnia 28
Chrysanthemum 30

To Adam

I picked a flower.
It was growing in my garden.

The flower I picked grew from a tiny seed.
I planted lots of little seeds in a long shallow hole many weeks ago.
I planted them in a sunny place.
I watered the seeds everyday.
In a short time small green plants poked their heads out of the ground.
Each day my plants grew a little bit taller and stronger.
Every few days I pulled out the weeds that grew around the plants.

One day I saw tiny buds on many of my plants.
Soon these grew into beautiful, perfect flowers.
> They were such vivid, bright colors.
> They felt like velvet.
> They made the air smell sweet and good.
> Cheerful, chirping birds came to see my gay flowers.
> Interesting insects came to drink their nectar.

My flowers were so lovely I picked one for you.

I PICKED A DAFFODIL!
What a cheerful sign of spring!
I know now that winter is gone for sure.
Daffodils are usually bright yellow, but there are white ones, too.
Daffodils have six petals.
In the center of each flower, standing higher than the petals, is a trumpet.
If the trumpet is shorter than the petals, it is called a cup.
Daffodils are grown from bulbs which are planted in the fall.
They bloom for only a short time in the spring.
There are daffodil farms on Long Island, and in Virginia, California, and Washington.
They specialize in growing daffodils for their bulbs.
These pretty flowers grow wild in parts of Europe and Asia.
The English poet William Wordsworth came upon a huge field of daffodils.
They inspired him to write:

"I wandered lonely as a cloud
That floats on high o'er vales and hills,
When all at once I saw a crowd,
A host of golden daffodils,
Beside the lake, beneath the trees,
Fluttering and dancing in the breeze."

I PICKED A ROSE!
>It is the most beautiful flower I have ever seen.
>Nature is a talented artist to have created such a flower.

The roses we love were developed over the years by gardeners and botanists.
There are hundreds of different kinds of roses.
Some roses grow close to the ground, some climb up fences and walls, and some grow on bushes.
Roses come in many shades and variations of red, white, yellow, orange, and pink.
Roses need a great deal of care.
They demand lots of water and a sunny spot to grow.
Roses are usually grown from small plants planted in the spring.
Many insects attack roses.
The sharp thorns on a rose plant help protect it from harm.

Perfume is often made from rose petals.
Oil taken from the petals is a common perfume base.
Thirty blossoms produce only about one drop of oil.
Thirty-two thousand flowers make about one pound of oil.

There are some interesting stories about roses.
>Cleopatra was supposed to have slept on a mattress stuffed with rose petals.
>She covered the floor of her palace with rose petals when entertaining Mark Antony.

I PICKED A DAISY!
It was growing in a field with hundreds and hundreds more dancing, white-petaled flowers.
What a wonderful sight!

I'll play a game with this daisy.
As I pull each petal off I'll say this rhyme:
"Richman, poorman, beggarman, thief,
Doctor, lawyer, merchant . . ."
I'm going to be a merchant!
I'll pick another daisy and try this test:
"He loves me, he loves me not.
He loves me, he loves me not."
How sad!   He doesn't love me.

Daisies grow wild as weeds in fields and meadows.
They make nice garden flowers, too.
If the soil is rich, you can have a lovely patch of daisies each spring.

There are many types of daisies.
There is the Shasta daisy, English daisy, and Michaelmas daisy.
Daisies can be red, yellow, or pink as well as white.
They always have a bright gold center.

I PICKED A TULIP!
It looks like a little, bright cup.
Tulips announce the arrival of spring.

Tulips have very good posture.
One bright flower stands tall and straight on each slender stem.
Tulips are grown from bulbs which are planted in the fall.
The bulb waits all winter under the ground for the warmth of spring before it sends its green sprouts up.
The name tulip comes from a Persian word which means turban.
Some people say it was named this because the flower looks like an upside-down turban.
Perhaps the name comes from the turban-wearing gardeners who raised tulips in Turkey long ago.
Travelers spread the news about these pretty flowers to other parts of Europe.
Tulips became very popular in Holland in the 17th century.
This popularity grew into a craze called Tulip Mania, which lasted from 1634 to 1637.
During this time tulips were so important that one bulb for a very rare flower sold for thousands of dollars.
Ever since the Tulip Mania Holland has been the leading producer of tulip bulbs.
There is a great variety of tulips.
Some are solid colors, while others are spotted or striped.
They can be red, purple, yellow, white, orange, rose, or gold.
Some tulips open widely while others keep a tight cup-shape.

I PICKED A GERANIUM!

    It was growing in a window box.
    There are many little red five-petaled flowers growing together on this stem.
    Together they make a geranium flower.
    This plant has large rounded leaves.

The geranium flower grows on a sturdy stem.
It is very often grown in pots on a porch or in a window box.
It grows well in gardens, too.
In warm climates the same plant will produce many flowers year after year.
In climates where there are cold winters the plant is brought in from the frost to keep warm until the next year's garden.

Geraniums first grew in Asia.
The early Indians of South America knew the geranium, too.
Today there are over 250 varieties of geraniums.

Geraniums grow best from *cuttings,* or pieces of stem cut off from a larger plant.
The cutting is left in water or moss until roots grow and it can be planted in soil.

You can have either red, pink, or white geraniums.
These flowers don't have a very pleasant smell.

I PICKED SOME SNAPDRAGONS!

There are many little snapdragons growing on a stem.
If you press the sides of a snapdragon flower together its little lips will snap open.
Just like an angry, snapping dragon.

These gay flowers originally grew near the Mediterranean Sea.
Today they grow almost everywhere.

Snapdragons are a favorite flower of bees.
They like its sweet nectar.
It makes good honey.

Snapdragons can be white, yellow, orange, pink, or red.
The stems grow to be about eighteen inches high.
These stems are not very strong and sometimes need to be propped up with a stick.
The height of the plants make them a good flower to grow along the back edges of your garden.

Snapdragons grow on their stems in a curious way.
There are always new flowers on the tips of the stem.
The further away you go from the end, the more wilted flowers you will find.
The flowers on the tips are always fresh.

I PICKED A PANSY!
    It has a little face.
    Spots of yellow, purple, and brown give the face a smile.
    These markings help guide insects to the flower's sweet nectar.

Pansies have rich, deep colors.
They come in almost any color you can imagine—from royal purple to rose, yellow, gold, light blue, and brown.

There are usually two or three colors on this five-petaled flower.
The petals feel so soft and smooth.

Pansies can be raised from seeds or from little plants.
If the soil is good they will grow into beautiful large flowers.
Pansies don't need too much care once they start to bloom.
Just a little water each day will do.

Another name for the pansy is heartsease.
Pansies are related to violets.

I PICKED A POPPY!

Its petals are as thin as tissue paper.
This one is beautiful red, but poppies come in pink or white, too.

You can make a poppy doll by turning the petals down for a skirt.
Tie them down with a blade of grass.
The center of the poppy makes a perfect head.
It will have a lacy collar, too.

Dried poppy seeds are small, black, and round.
They are delicious on bread and rolls.

The nectar from certain poppies forms a black gum called opium.
Morphine comes from this gum, too.
Opium and morphine are dangerous, but very valuable drugs.
Morphine is an excellent pain reliever when taken under doctor's orders.

I PICKED SOME LILIES OF THE VALLEY!
  There are many small bell-shaped white flowers growing together on a stem.
  They smell so sweet and look so pretty.

Lilies of the valley are *perennials,* or flowers that bloom each year.

Lilies of the valley come up in April and May.

The flowers last only a short time, but the green leaves stay fresh all summer long.

The plants grow to be only five or six inches tall.

They grow easily in sun or shade.

A small bed of lilies of the valley will soon become a large one without much attention.

The plants spread because of their creeping underground roots.

Lilies of the valley are members of the lily family.

They are a favorite flower for brides' bouquets.

Lilies of the valley are known to some people as May lilies and Our Lady's tears.

I PICKED A SUNFLOWER!
>It's a giant flower.
>The biggest I've ever picked.
>It has bright yellow petals and a round brown center.
>It must be a rather smart flower because it turns its head to follow the sun.
>Few flowers do this.
>You must watch it very carefully to see this happen.

Sunflowers grow wild in parts of the Middle West.
Some are planted from seeds in gardens.
They are so common in Kansas that it is known as the Sunflower State.
Sunflowers do best in hot sun.
Some grow as high as fifteen feet and have flowers one foot in diameter.

The flat gray and white sunflower seeds are good to eat when roasted.
Birds like them, too.
Oil is made from sunflower seeds.
This oil is used to make soap and paint.
In some places in Europe cattle eat the leaves of the sunflower plant and the stems are burned as fuel.

Many sunflowers growing together make a fine, tall hedge.

I PICKED A ZINNIA!
    It is a gay and sturdy flower.
    Many, many little overlapping petals make up one flower.
    It is a cousin to the giant sunflower I just picked.

Zinnias are an easy flower to grow.
They like both sun and shade.
They bloom all summer.
The more zinnias you pick for a pretty bouquet, the more will grow.
They stay fresh in water for many days.

Zinnias are native to North and South America.
They were named for the 18th century German botanist, Johann Gottifried Zinn.
Zinn came to Mexico to collect plants and seeds.
He helped make the zinnia a good garden flower.

Some zinnias are as small as plums and others are as big as grapefruit.

I PICKED A CHRYSANTHEMUM!
Now fall must be near.
This feathery flower comes with the end of summer.
Chrysanthemums make beautiful football corsages.

Chrysanthemums have bloomed in the gardens of Japan and China for hundreds of years.
They are the national flower of Japan.

Although it is a popular Oriental flower, we know it by a Greek name.
Gold in Greek is *chrysos* and *anthos* means flower.
Yellow or gold are the most common colors for chrysanthemums.
They do appear in white, red, bronze, orange, lavender, and pink, as well.
For short, chrysanthemums are called "mums."

Chrysanthemums are a hardy flower.
They should be planted in the spring for fall blooms.
They like a sunny, well-drained spot.
A bouquet of chrysanthemums will last many, many days when kept in fresh water.

About the author

Sharon Lerner's published works combine her love of nature, art, and writing. As an artist, Mrs. Lerner has been recognized for her watercolors, collages and jewelry. She has a degree in art education from the University of Minnesota and has been a lecturer and guide at the Walker Art Center and the Minneapolis Institute of Arts. She has taught at University High School, Walker Art Center, and the White Bear Public School System. An experienced writer, Mrs. Lerner is the author of *Places of Musical Fame*, *The Self-Portrait in Art*, *I Found a Leaf*, *I Like Vegetables*, *I Picked a Flower*, *Who Will Wake Up Spring?*, *Square is a Shape*, *Orange is a Color* and *Straight is a Line*. She resides in Minneapolis with her husband and three children.